JON SCIESZKA'S TRUCKTOWN

PETE'S PARTY

WRITTEN BY JON SCIESZKA

CHARACTERS AND ENVIRONMENTS DEVELOPED BY THE

dESiGN garage

DAVID SHANNON   LOREN LONG   DAVID GORDON

ILLUSTRATION CREW:

Executive producer: TOT INDUSTRIES in association with Animagic S.L.

Creative supervisor: Sergio Pablos ◦ Drawings by: Juan Pablo Navas ◦ Color by: Isabel Nadal

Color assistant: Gabriela Lazbal ◦ Art director: Karin Paprocki

READY-TO-ROLL

ALADDIN PAPERBACKS
NEW YORK   LONDON   TORONTO   SYDNEY

🐘 ALADDIN PAPERBACKS

An imprint of Simon & Schuster Children's Publishing Division

1230 Avenue of the Americas, New York, NY 10020

The text of this book was set in Truck King.

Manufactured in the United States of America

First Aladdin Paperbacks edition June 2008

10 9 8 7 6 5 4 3

Library of Congress Cataloging-in-Publication Data

Scieszka, Jon.

Pete's party / by Jon Scieszka ; artwork created by the Design Garage:

David Gordon, Loren Long, David Shannon.—1st Aladdin Paperbacks ed.

p. cm.—(Jon Scieszka's Trucktown. Ready-to-roll)

Summary: The Trucktown trucks follow the road signs directing them to Pete's party.

ISBN-13: 978-1-4169-4138-5   ISBN-10: 1-4169-4138-X (pbk)

ISBN-13: 978-1-4169-4149-1   ISBN-10: 1-4169-4149-5 (library)

[1. Traffic signs and signals—Fiction. 2. Trucks—Fiction.] I. Design Garage.

II. Gordon, David, 1965 Jan. 22- ill. III. Long, Loren, ill.

IV. Shannon, David, ill. V. Title.

PZ7.S41267Pe 2008   [E]—dc22   2007027154

"How do we get there?"
"Follow the signs."

"Do you want an ice cream?
Do you want an ice cream?
Do you want an ice cream?"

"Now how do we get home?"

"Follow the **Signs**."

HSCEX   +
         E
         SCIES

SCIESZKA, JON
    PETE'S PARTY

SCENIC WOODS
05/09